MRAC

HARBINGERS 9

Leviathan

Bill Myers

**Frank Peretti, Angela Hunt,
and Alton Gansky**

D0841441

JAN – – 2017

BILL MYERS

Published by Amaris Media International.
Copyright © 2015 Bill Myers
Cover Design: Angela Hunt
Photo ©Alexei Novikov

All rights reserved. No part of this book may be reproduced, stored in a retrieval system, or transmitted in any form or by any other means—electronic, mechanical, photocopy, recording, or any other—except for brief quotations in printed reviews, without prior permission from the publisher.

ISBN: 0692565558
ISBN-10: 978-0692565551

For more information, visit us on Facebook:
https://www.facebook.com/pages/Harbingers/705107309586877

or www.harbingersseries.com.

HARBINGERS

A novella series by
Bill Myers, Frank Peretti, Angela Hunt, and Alton Gansky

In this fast-paced world with all its demands, the four of us wanted to try something new. Instead of the longer novel format, we wanted to write something equally as engaging but that could be read in one or two sittings—on the plane, waiting to pick up the kids from soccer, or as an evening's read.

We also wanted to play. As friends and seasoned novelists, we thought it would be fun to create a game we could participate in together. The rules were simple:

Rule #1

Each of us would write as if we were one of the characters in the series:

Bill Myers would write as Brenda, the street-hustling tattoo artist who sees images of the future.

Frank Peretti would write as the professor, the atheist ex-priest ruled by logic.

Angela Hunt would write as Andi, the professor's brilliant-but-geeky assistant who sees inexplicable patterns.

Alton Gansky would write as Tank, the naïve, big-hearted jock with a surprising connection to a healing power.

Rule #2

Instead of the four of us writing one novella together (we're friends but not crazy), we would write it like a TV series. There would be an overarching story line into which we'd plug our individual novellas, with each story written from our character's point of view.

If you're keeping track, this is the order:

Harbingers #1—*The Call*—Bill Myers
Harbingers #2—*The Haunted*—Frank Peretti
Harbingers #3—*The Sentinels*—Angela Hunt
Harbingers #4—*The Girl*—Alton Gansky

Volumes #1-4 omnibus: *Cycle One: Invitation*

Harbingers #5—*The Revealing*—Bill Myers
Harbingers #6—*Infestation*—Frank Peretti
Harbingers #7—*Infiltration*—Angela Hunt
Harbingers #8—*The Fog*—Alton Gansky

Volumes #5-8 omnibus: *Cycle Two: Mosaic*

Harbingers #9—*Leviathan*—Bill Myers

There you have it—at least for now. We hope you'll find these as entertaining in the reading as we are in the writing.

Bill, Frank, Angie, and Al

Chapter 1

"You okay?"

Daniel said nothing. No surprise there. Just kept starin' out the window of the plane. But the workout he was givin' the napkin in his hand said somethin' was up.

I motion to the hills across the city. "Check it out. That's the Hollywood sign over there."

Nothing. Vintage Daniel.

We were a minute or so from landing so I capped my pen and closed the sketch pad. I'd been drawing some sort of octopus thing. In the old days it would have been for somebody's tattoo. Not now. Now the stuff I see in my head has nothing to do with tatting somebody's future . . . and everything to do with our group's assignments.

The plane shuttered and jerked. Not a big deal. 'Cept I'd be more comfortable if Daniel hadn't muttered something.

"What's that?" I said.

He stayed glued to the window and repeated it. Something like *Leviathan*, whatever that means.

The plane bucked harder. I sucked in my breath. Me and flying aren't the best of friends. Though you wouldn't know it by the free miles I've been racking up.

None of us knows who's footing the bill for these flights, or paying the expenses when we get there. But we got ideas. For starters, they're the good guys. Least that's what we hope. And they're fighting off what we think are the bad guys—something called *The Gate*—a group that's got lots of nasty ideas and nasty dudes . . . some that aren't so human.

Course we got some unearthly types on our side, too. Seems more than just our world is interested in what's going on down here.

The plane leaped again and dropped—this time a couple seconds. Enough for people to shout and scream. 'Cept Daniel. He just kept lookin' out the window. Only now his lips were movin' a mile a minute. I can't hear words, but I know he's praying. Or talkin' to his imaginary friends (who we're findin' out aren't always so imaginary).

Another drop.

"Daniel!"

He reached out and took my hand. A nice, sweet gesture . . . before we die.

More bucking and falling. The screams became non-stop.

Out the window I saw a freeway with cars—so

close we could touch 'em. The plane's engines revved hard, throwing me back into the seat. The pilot was gunning it, trying to reach the runway.

The whole plane banged like we hit something. But we were still picking up speed, folks screamin', some cryin' out to sweet Jesus for mercy. A second later and we slammed into the ground. I got thrown forward, seat belt digging into my gut. The engines shrieked, reversing thrust. The plane shook and shimmered like a car with bad brakes.

But we were down. And in pretty good shape— 'cept for the weeping and swearing . . . and the smell of vomit across the aisle.

Daniel leaned back into the seat and closed his eyes.

I took a swallow and turned to him. "We good?"

He nodded. Took a deep breath and blew it out.

I did, too.

The pilot came on, all apologies. Something about wind sheers that may or may not be true. Who knows? Who cares. I stole another look to Daniel, his face all wet and shiny, but he seemed relaxed.

I let go of his hand, wiped my palms, and took another breath. Long and slow.

Just another day at the office.

Chapter 2

"Brenda!"

I braced myself as Cowboy, aka Tank, threw his grizzly-bear arms around me. (I'm as fond of hugging as I am flying). We'd had plenty of talks about boundaries, but the big fellow could never quite seem to get it. And to be honest, with our last few assignments, I felt less and less inclined to remind him. I was changin'. Guess we all were.

"You're late, Barnick," the professor barked. He's also part of the team. But if he's changin', he's doing a lot better job at keeping it hidden.

"Professor, you can't blame them for the airline being late." That's Andi Goldstein. If the professor was the team's Eeyore, Andi, his bubbly, red-headed assistant, was our Tigger. But a whole lot smarter— 'specially when it comes to computers and in seeing patterns just about everywhere.

The man grunted and headed for the doors. "Limo is waiting."

I turned to Andi. "Bad day?"

She shrugged. "With him, who can tell?"

We headed out of the terminal. After Mr. Toad's Wild Ride on the plane, what I wouldn't give for a smoke. But we were late and there was no way the professor was going to wait.

Outside it was typical LA—noise, busses, taxies. And people. Way too many for my tastes. It's not that I'm anti-social it's, well, let's just say the sun ain't the only reason I like livin' in the desert.

We followed the professor to a stretch limo waiting at the curb and climbed inside. Memories of our last gig, the one with the fog creepies in San Diego, came to mind. Needless to say, I hoped this mission would be a lot safer.

"So what's up?" I slipped off my backpack as the driver shut the door. "And why all the urgency? They gave us less than twenty-four hours this time."

No one had an answer, which was pretty typical. 'Course we could refuse and decline any time we wanted, but they (whoever 'they' were) knew we wouldn't. The mystery and excitement was just too much for us. Like it or not, we'd become adventure junkies.

We always complained. But we never declined.

I glanced to Daniel. He'd already settled in, making himself comfortable playing one of his blow-'em-up app games.

"You know that will rot his brain," the professor said.

I ignored the man. A good tactic when I could pull

it off.

Andi read from her tablet. "This came in just before you landed: 'Today, 2:00 PM, Everbright Studios invites you and your party to be our guest for a VIP viewing of the final rehearsal and taping of the new reality TV show, *Live or Die, the Ultimate Reality.*'"

"A television show?" I said. "We've come all this way for a television show?"

Andi kept reading. "After a brief break, followed by a gourmet dinner with cast and crew, you will be escorted to front row seats for the 7:00 PM taping."

I frowned. "And our purpose?"

She shook her head. "This is all we have."

I threw a glance to the professor. I now saw why the resident control freak was a bit cranky.

"And this limo?" I asked.

"The show's executive producer—" Andi glanced back to her tablet— "a Mr. Norman Anderson, ordered it for us."

"But why?"

Always the optimist, Cowboy chimed in. "Guess we'll just have to wait 'til we get there. But a TV show, that'll be kinda fun, right?"

Fun wasn't exactly the word that came to mind. Like it or not, I was already catching the professor's negativity—something I wasn't thrilled about.

"Hey, check it out." Cowboy scooted to the closest window. "Look at them cool pillars."

Outside there were a bunch of big plastic pillars along the roadway. All different sizes. Even in the afternoon sun, you could see they were lit inside by colored lights that were changing . . . from purple . . . to green . . . to red.

"The LAX Pylons," Andi said. She went back to

her tablet and looked up something.

Cowboy pulled out his cell phone, made a quick pan across our faces, and began videotaping the pillars out the window.

Andi found a link and began to read: "Originally constructed in the year 2000, the pillars range from twenty-five to sixty feet tall. They were designed to give the feeling of taking off in an airplane. They culminate in a circle of fifteen, 100-foot columns which represent the fifteen city council districts, while simultaneously bringing to mind ancient sights such as Stonehenge." She paused and looked out the window. "Pretty neat art, huh?

I didn't know what to say.

The professor did. "How much?"

"What's that?"

"The price tag? What was the expenditure for this "neat art?"

She glanced at her tablet. "Fifteen million dollars."

He looked back out the window and muttered, "Welcome to Los Angeles."

A moment later the TV monitor in the back blasted on. It was a scene from the first *Superman* movie. It only lasted a couple seconds, then went off. I glanced to Daniel. Then to Cowboy. Nobody had touched the controls.

"Well," the professor said, "that was certainly—"

The TV came on again. This time it was one of those old *Rocky* movies.

"Andi?" The professor said.

It went off.

"I'm on it." She scooted to the control console and examined the glowing buttons.

The monitor came back on again. Longer. It was

that weird Leonardo DeCaprio movie with the spinning top.

Then off.

"Andrea!" The professor repeated.

"I don't—"

Then back on. Some British sci-fi thing with a flying telephone booth.

And off.

Cowboy and Daniel moved over to help her.

Then on. I recognized this one immediately. It was a scene from the first *Hunger Games.*

Then off.

The professor grabbed the limo phone and spoke into it. "Driver, will you please—"

Back on again, drowning out his voice. It was some cartoon with talking ants.

And off.

"—but surely, you have a master control up there that—"

And on. Another *Rocky* movie. Newer.

Andi scooted from the console and rummaged through what looked like a silverware drawer.

The *Rocky* movie went off.

The professor kept speaking to the driver. "I find your ignorance comparable only to your—"

And on. Back to the *Superman* movie.

A moment later the professor slammed down the phone. The TV switched back to the first *Rocky* movie.

Andi pulled a steak knife from the drawer and slid back to the console. She began attacking its tiny screws with the tip of the knife.

The spinning top movie came back on.

"Andrea!"

"Patience, Professor. Patien—"

Then we were back to the British sci-fi thing.

She kept working on the screws until she was able to pull out the control panel, guts and all. But the TV still kept playing.

The Hunger Games was back on.

She stared dubiously at the attached wires.

The ant cartoon came on.

Then the newer *Rocky* movie.

She sighed, then gave the control panel a good yank, ripping out all the wires. The television went off. This time for good.

We sat in silence. Blessed silence. Except for Cowboy, who was never able to endure any silence for too long. "Well, that was weird, huh?"

None of us disagreed.

Chapter 3

"Hold positions, please. Camera Three, that's your hero shot. Two and Four, stay wide."

"Got it."

"Staying wide."

We stood way in the back of some state-of-the-art TV control room. A dozen people in headsets with faces lit by twice that many monitors and a long board of glowing lights and flashing buttons. Techno-geek heaven.

Andi loved it.

The fact that we got headsets to listen in made it all the better.

A couple hours earlier, our limo had pulled onto the studio lot. We were greeted by a perky blonde, complete with Barbie figure and brilliantly white, glow-in-the-dark teeth.

"Hi there," she said as we climbed out and stretched our legs. "My name is Ashlee. I'm so glad you could make it. So how was your flight? Terrific, I hope."

"Howdy, I'm Tank," Cowboy said, giving her his good ol' boy grin. "Me, Andi and the professor here, ours was great. But Brenda and the little guy, I guess theirs wasn't so hot."

"Oh, I'm sorry to hear that," Ashlee said.

I reached back inside to grab my backpack.

"Oh, don't worry about that." She blinded us with another one of her smiles. "We'll have that delivered to your hotel."

"Right." I lugged the pack out and onto my shoulder. "I'll just hang onto it." Old street habits die hard.

"Rehearsal has already started," Ashlee said, "but I'm sure we can slip you into—oh, here's Skylar now." She motioned to an approaching clone of herself. Different hair, same teeth, and anatomically impossible figure. "She'll escort you through the studio and up to the control room. "

"Hi there." The clone smiled. "My name is Skylar. I'm so glad you could make it. So how was your flight? Terrific, I hope."

I traded looks with Andi. Can anybody say, *Stepford Wives*?

Cowboy didn't notice. "Hi, I'm Tank. Ours was great. But Miss Brenda's and Daniel's, here, theirs wasn't so good."

"Oh, I'm sorry to hear it."

"So, Skylar," Ashlee said. "We're running a bit late. Would you mind escorting our guests to the control room?"

"Why, I'd love to, Ashlee. If you'll join me and walk this way, please." She turned and we started toward what looked like a giant airplane hanger.

The professor sped up and joined her. "Excuse me, Miss?"

She turned her perma-smile on him. "Yes?"

"What exactly is our purpose here?"

"Oh, that's easy. You're here because our executive producer, Norman Anderson, invited you. Didn't you receive his E-vite?"

"Yes, we did, but he failed to mention why."

"Oh. Because we're taping his new reality show, *Live or Die, the Ultimate Reality.*

"I appreciate that, but the question still remains—why?"

"Because you're his invited guests."

He took a measured breath and tried again. "I understand the name of the show and I understand we are his invited guests, but you have yet to address the question of *why?*"

She looked at him blankly. Then apparently guessing he was hard of hearing, she raised her voice. "Because we're taping his new reality show, *Live or Die, the Ultimate Reality!*"

The professor opened his mouth, then closed it. It was obvious he didn't know how to communicate with her species.

When we got to the main entrance, Skylar turned to us. "Now we'll have to be very quiet." She looked to the professor. "As Mr. Anderson's *invited guests* you are being allowed inside the control room. That's quite an honor, but it will require that you turn off your cell phones and remain completely silent. Is that understood?"

Everyone nodded except for the professor.

She repeated louder for his benefit, *"Is that understood?"*

"Yes." Andi stepped in before he could respond. "We understand."

Skylar flashed one last smile for the road and opened the door. We stepped inside and were struck by a wave of coldness. The edges of the room were dark, but you could see it was huge—a couple hundred feet wide, forty, fifty feet tall. In the center was a big oval sand pit. It was surrounded by a fake stone wall and fake stone bleachers, eight, maybe ten rows high.

"Welcome to the Coliseum," Skylar proudly said. "It's like the Roman Coliseum—you know, the one they have in Rome, Italy? Only it's not as big. It's a lot smaller because it's not as big. It's a miniature version."

"Of the one in Rome, Italy?" the professor asked. We all caught his sarcasm. Well, most of us.

"That's right!" Skylar beamed. "Exactly."

We kept walking.

As we approached the side wall I could see half a dozen TV cameras mounted around it. Another one hung from a cable over the pit, and two more were manned by live operators inside the pit. Each and every camera was focused on two people; a young man and a young woman. They pretended to fight, but in slow motion.

"Are those the stars?" Cowboy whispered.

Skylar shook her head. "They're what we in the business call 'stand ins.' They're to help the director find the best angles for when the real fight begins this evening."

"Which brings me back to my original question," the professor said. "Why have we been selected to—"

"Oh, there's Brittani." Our guide waved to another perfectly proportioned assistant waiting at the top of the bleachers. She stood next to a large, black room with mirrored windows on the front. Skylar started up the steps and we followed.

Andi leaned over and whispered to me. "Don't these girls ever eat?"

"If they do," I said, "it all goes to their boobs."

We arrived and the new girl flashed her mandatory grin. "Hi, there. My name is Brittani. I'm so glad you could make it. How was your flight? I hope it was terrific."

Now, for over an hour, we'd been standing (as in not sitting) inside the back of that big black room watching and listening to some overweight Jabba-the-Hut director firing off instructions to his camera crew. Other than us, the only person standing was some lean, older guy in a buzz cut. By the way he paced, chewed gum, and sipped his Starbuck Grande, you could tell he was in charge. I'm guessing, he was the mysterious Norman Anderson.

"Hold right there," the director said into his headset.

On the monitors, the two stand-in actors froze. Since we'd been there, they'd gone from slow motion punching, to slow motion sword play, to slow motion battle maces, to slow motion lances. If it had been real, it would have been way too gross for Daniel. But everything was fake . . . including the fake blood smeared over the guy's face when he was fake-stabbed in the eye before it was fake gouged out.

For the past few minutes, the girl was supposedly getting the worst of it. Her hand had been fake cut off by a cleaver—same fake blood, only now it spurted from a pump in her sleeve. And a few seconds ago, her ear had been fake sliced off.

"Beautiful," the director said. "Okay, Sean, take the butt of your sword and slam it into Jillian's face."

The actor nodded and, in slow motion, spun around and pretended to hit the girl's face.

"Jillian, drop to the ground. You're dazed."

She lowered to her knees and rolled over.

"Fantastic. Cameras Two and Three, don't forget to go for cleavage. With all that rolling around I want plenty."

The assistant next to him asked, "What about wardrobe malfunction?"

The director chuckled. "Let's hope."

The others joined in as if on cue.

"Okay, Sean, grab the ax off the back wall there, and come after her. Camera One and Two, go tight but give him room."

The images on the monitors shifted as the actor scooped up the ax and came toward the girl.

"Slower . . ."

He slowed.

"Raise it over your head."

He did.

"Everyone check your marks. This is the kill shot." He turned to Anderson, who paced behind him and nodded. He turned back to the monitors. "Alright. Gore lights, please."

The lights in the arena turned deep red.

"Strobe."

They began flashing.

"Camera Two, go for the money shot. Extreme close up. I doubt he'll stop at one blow, so stay in there, nice and tight for spurting blood. We'll have the cameras watertight by tonight." He laughed. "Make that, 'blood-tight.'"

Smiles all around.

"Alright people, let's wrap this puppy and go on break."

Both actors nodded. Sean slowly brought down the ax until it hovered an inch from the girl's face.

"Good. And repeat."

He raised the ax and brought it down again.

"Good."

"What if it flips?" the assistant asked. "What if the girl wins?"

"Then we'll adjust. This is just practice." He spoke back into the headset. "Okay, Sean, keep hacking. Don't stop until I call."

The stand in nodded and pretended to hit Jillian again, then again, and—

Suddenly all the monitors flickered. For a second another show came on. Not a TV show, but a scene from the *Superman* movie. The same one that had come on in the limo.

The director shouted "What the—"

The monitors all flickered to a *Rocky* movie. The same part we'd seen in the limo. Then the Leonardo DiCaprio spinning top.

We all traded looks.

Anderson slammed his Starbucks cup down on a console near us. "Engineering!"

"On it." Some shaved-headed guy moved into action.

Next, we saw the show with the flying telephone booth. Then the scene from *The Hunger Games*.

The director swore—worse than me on a bad day.

The scene switched to the ant cartoon. Then the newer *Rocky* movie.

It was exactly like our limo ride. Except for one added bonus: The Starbuck Grande beside us? No one touched it. No one was near it. But, suddenly, for no reason at all, it exploded.

Chapter 4

"And we're here because . . ." One thing about the professor—he's as persistent as he is obnoxious. At least this time we were with someone whose teeth didn't look Photoshopped and who actually had answers.

Norman Anderson was eating dinner with us and the rest of his crew in the studio cafeteria—if you call a "cafeteria" someplace where they serve prime rib, salmon, and plenty of veggie things for the veggie-heads.

Anderson barely glanced up from his steak to

answer the professor. "You're kidding, right?"

"Do I look like I'm kidding?"

The lean, fifty-somethinger sized up the professor, then went back to eating. "You're here because I'm a man who can't say no to his daughter."

We traded looks. Clueless as ever.

He glanced back up and saw our expressions. "What? Helsa didn't tell you?"

The name stopped us cold.

"Helsa . . ." Cowboy said.

"Yeah. She and my daughter are like best friends." He spotted a waitress who didn't quite measure up to Team Barbie, and signaled her to refill his water. Perrier, of course.

He turned back to Cowboy who still had his mouth open. "You're the football player, right?"

"Was," Cowboy corrected. "But how do you—"

"And Helsa, she's your niece or something?"

Before Cowboy could correct him—little details like they were totally unrelated and Helsa was just a friend sent from a parallel world to sometimes help us—the professor cut him off. "Yes, she's his niece."

"Professor," Cowboy protested, "that ain't exactly the—"

"Close enough." The professor turned back to Anderson. "It's a rather long and boring story."

The man didn't notice or care. He went back to his steak. "So for months she's been telling my kid that you and your pals here have been dying to come onto a real Hollywood set. You know, see how things are done."

We traded more looks.

He took a sip of his water, stifled a burp, and set the glass down. "And since you were already in the area—vacation is it?—I figured, why not? I mean if it makes my daughter happy."

"Are they here?" Andi asked, glancing around. "Helsa? Your daughter?"

"Right," he scoffed. "Like I'd let them see a show like this. I sent them with the wife to Maui for the week." He turned back to Cowboy. "Cute kid, your niece. Strange, but cute."

It was about then I noticed the water in Anderson's glass rippling. Like someone bumped the table. But when I looked at the other glasses they were perfectly still.

It was the professor's turn to scoff. "You refuse to expose your own child to the violence of your show and yet you are perfectly willing to present it to the entire nation?"

Anderson gave him a look. It was obvious they weren't going to be friends. "Do you know anything about network ratings?"

"Not a thing."

"If you did, you'd know that everything's in the toilet. Nothing's making money these days."

"So you're producing this type of barbaric ilk simply to make a—"

"This is the real world, Professor. Not some Ivy League hot house. People here have to work to eat."

"Even if it means prostituting themselves?" The professor kept pushing buttons, one of his specialties.

"If someone's got the money and is willing to foot the bill, yeah, I'm willing to help them spend it."

I glanced back at Anderson's water. It was rippling harder.

Always the peacemaker, Andi cooled things down by asking, "When you say, 'foot the bill,' are you referring to the network? To your sponsors?"

"For starters."

"Starters?"

"There are other players. No one talks much about them; they prefer to avoid the spotlight. But we all know they're there and that they've got major bucks. Truth is, every year they're investing a bit more."

"Into programs as uplifting as yours," the professor said.

"The show was not created in a vacuum."

"Meaning?"

"They came to me. Not with every detail, of course. They trust my creative genius. But the initial concept was theirs."

"And you took their money for services rendered."

"I wasn't thrilled about it, but look at the country. You'd have to be an idiot not to see this is where programs are going. This is what people want for entertainment, so this is what they'll get." Anderson returned to cutting his steak, none too gently.

After a moment I asked, "These other people, with the money, they got a name?"

"Like I said, they like to be anonymous."

"But you know who they are."

"I've seen a contract or two.

"And?"

He looked up at me, then to the others. Obviously figuring it didn't matter, he returned to his steak. "They call themselves the Gate."

If we'd been surprised about Helsa, we were downright stunned about this.

Anderson didn't notice, but kept eating. After a moment, he quoted, "'For better or worse the influence of the church has been usurped by film.

Films and television tell us what is right and wrong.'"

"They said that?" Cowboy asked. "The Gate?"

Anderson shook his head. "George Lucas. But they quote it. They're big fans of using the media to 'educate' and 'enlighten.'"

"By reveling in sex and violence," the professor said.

Anderson had had enough. He laid down his knife and fork and shoved away his plate. Leaning into the professor, he said, "It's called entertainment. We give the people what they want. No one takes it seriously."

"Actually—" Andi cleared her throat as she pulled out her tablet and snapped it on. "There are over 300 studies directly linking TV violence to social violence. More studies than link smoking to lung cancer."

Anderson turned to her, unsure how to respond.

"She's kinda smart," Cowboy said.

Searching for a link, she continued, "In fact, a 1992 article in *The Journal of the American Medical Association* concluded—" she kept looking— "ah, here it is: 'Long-term childhood exposure to television is a casual factor behind approximately one half of the homicides committed in the United States, or approximately 10,000 homicides annually.'"

Anderson frowned.

Cowboy grinned. "I told you."

She kept reading. "'If television technology had never been developed, there would today be 10,000 fewer homicides each year in the United States, 70,000 fewer rapes, and 700,000 fewer injurious assaults.'"

I glanced to Anderson's glass. The ripples had grown so strong the water was sloshing back and forth.

"Right." He grabbed his napkin, wiped his mouth and started to rise. "Well, like I said, it's a living."

"Pretending to kill people?" the professor said.

"Pretending? *Pretending?* No my friend, what you see tonight will not be pretend. It will be the real thing. *Live or Die, the Ultimate Reality.*"

"You mean you're gonna kill someone right there on TV?" Cowboy asked.

"We'll have disclaimers. Viewer discretion, late night viewing, the usual."

"But—"

"The actors have signed wavers. Everyone knows what they're getting into."

"And you seriously believe people will tune in to watch?" Andi asked.

"Just like they did in the Roman Coliseum," he said. "Just like we do at freeway accidents. Sure, we pretend to wring our hands when we pass by, say we hope no one got hurt . . . but we slow our cars, hoping against hope that we'll see something awful."

No one had a comeback.

He turned to leave.

But I had one last question. "And your live audience? You think they're just gonna sit around and watch someone get snuffed?"

He turned back to me. "I wouldn't worry about that, missy. They're going to have a little help."

"Help?"

He didn't bother to answer. "So you don't miss any of the action, I'll make sure you have front row seats. Now, if you'll excuse me, I have a few hundred fires to put out before the show—which you just might find entertaining . . . in spite of yourself."

He turned and walked away—just as his water

glass toppled over on the table and crashed to the floor.

Chapter 5

What I saw next was pretty violent. So if you want to skip over this chapter and go to the next, no hard feelings. I'll fill you in later. 'Specially if you're like under seventeen or something. I'm serious. Fact is, if I wasn't part of all this, I'd of skipped the whole show. But like someone somewhere said, "If you're gonna fight evil, sometimes you gotta look it in the eye."

That was the very argument we had about going back inside and seeing the show. I was sayin', "I've seen enough violence in my life. I don't need no more."

The others might have agreed with me . . . if it wasn't for the professor. As strange as it sounds, he was the one that kept insisting we go.

"Why's it so important to you?" I demanded.

"What it is to me is entirely irrelevant. But it's abundantly clear the Gate is behind much of this.

Equally clear is the fact that we have been sent here, at no little expense, to deal with it.

"And don't forget Helsa," Cowboy added. "She's in on this, too."

"Yes." The professor cleared his throat. The girl was never one of his favorite topics. "The point is, great pains have been taken to arrange this encounter. It would be both illogical and irresponsible for us to simply walk away from it."

He looked at me for a comeback, but he had a point. I hated to admit it cause it was getting to be a habit.

He continued. "But not young Daniel here. You can load him up with all the vile video games you want, but I will not allow him to see this."

"Oh, *you'll* not allow him?" I said. "What, are you his guardian now?"

"I could do no worse than you.

He was right . . . again. Two for two. I let it go, hoping I wasn't losing my touch.

An hour later, one of the Barbies was babysitting Daniel somewhere else on the lot, while the rest of us sat in the front row of the arena. The place was packed. Three hundred spectators waiting for the show. They had no idea what it was, but it was free, so here they were.

"Where's Andi?" Cowboy asked. "Why isn't she—oh, there you are."

"Where have you been?" the professor asked as she took her seat.

She motioned to the control room up behind us. "Checking their equipment. Looking for that glitch."

"And?"

"We couldn't find a thing. But they did offer me a job."

"They *what?*"

"Relax, Professor. I didn't take it. Though their equipment is breathtaking. Real state of the art." She opened a small, plastic case and took out what looked like fancy ear plugs. There were four sets. "Here," she said, passing them out to us.

"What are they? Cowboy asked.

"They're like noise cancellation headphones, but smaller. They go inside the ear."

"It's gonna get that loud?" Cowboy said.

She shook her head. "It's not about the volume. It's something else. Some sort of filtering device. All the crew wear them."

The professor looked at his doubtfully. "And what exactly do they filter out?"

Andi motioned back to the control room. "The engineer says it's some sort of high frequency they'll be broadcasting through the studio. Something about—"

"Ladies and Gentlemen . . ." The announcer's voice echoed through the building. "Welcome to the world premier of . . . *Live or Die, the Ultimate Reality!*"

The applause signs overhead flashed and the crowd clapped and cheered.

The contestants were introduced. Not the stand-ins, but the real people . . . a perfectly cut, shirtless piece of eye candy in shorts, glistening in oil. And his opponent, some chick, an obvious supporter of the steroid industry, with skimpy shorts and a halter so tiny you wondered why she even bothered.

They stood at opposite ends of the arena, huffing

and puffing, getting themselves all worked up . . . right along with the crowd . . . and me, just a little. Seriously. I mean I knew better, but it was like their enthusiasm was contagious.

The announcer continued: "Each of you have your weapons. Choose what you wish, any time you wish. And remember, there are no rules! Anything and everything goes!"

The crowd cheered, hooting and hollering their approval. And I felt myself getting pulled right along with them. Not much. But enough.

"You have no referees. No score keepers. The only way to win is to be the last one standing . . . the last one whose heart is still beating!"

The cheering grew louder.

"Because ladies and gentlemen: This *is* . . THE . . . ULTIMATE . . . REALITY!"

Lights flashed, music blared and I was clapping along with everyone else. Well, almost everyone. Andi, Cowboy, and the professor sat there like lumps on a log.

"Come on!" I shouted to them. "It's only a show!"

An air horn blasted and the fight began.

The kid was the first to attack. He grabbed a battle ax off his wall of weapons and raced at the girl. But she was no wimp. She grabbed a broadsword from her wall and spun around just in time to block him. The clang of steel filled the arena. He swung again and she blocked again. Then again. You could literally see the sparks.

The crowd was on their feet. There was something so real. So honest and brutal.

Blow after blow came. First he had the advantage. Then she did. Then he . . . as they went from weapon to weapon. What she lacked in strength, she made up for in speed. What he lacked in agility, he made up for in raw power.

They were so equally matched that at first there was no blood. But as they wore each other down they got tired, sloppy. The first real wound came when they were both using swords. She managed to get a good one right across that handsome face of his. I gasped along with the crowd, then joined in the applause.

It got even more interesting when he attacked her with a short lance. She countered, holding him off with the sword once, twice. Then she misjudged. He sank his spear deep into her thigh. If she screamed, you couldn't hear over our shouting.

Then, to everyone's amazement, she broke the spear. Snapped it off right there, leaving a piece still in her leg. More cheers. But that was nothing compared to when she reached down and yanked out that remaining piece. Blood gushed everywhere. The crowd went wild. It got even better when she ripped off her glove and stuffed part of it into the wound to stop the bleeding.

She limped back to her wall and grabbed the broadsword . . . then came at him with everything she had.

"Yes!" I shouted. "Go! Go!"

She swung hard. The kid barely dodged it. She missed his chest, but as the sword came down, she did manage to cut off two of his toes. More blood. The crowd went nuts.

"Yes!" I shouted. "Yes!"

"Brenda . . ."

I looked down to see Andi tugging at my arm. I

shook her lose.

Now it was the kid's turn. He limped to his wall and grabbed one of those iron balls on a chain with spikes. He turned and staggered toward her.

But the girl wasn't backing down. She'd lost a lot of blood, and was still bleeding, but there was no way she was gonna run.

He came at her, swinging the ball. She ducked, the pointed spikes barely missing her. He swung it around again. This time she wasn't so lucky. The spikes missed her neck, but caught her arm, digging into the flesh.

She screamed, staggered backwards, fighting to stay on her feet. But it was obvious things were coming to an end.

The crowd began chanting. "Kill! Kill! Kill!"

He came at her again . . . swinging. She ducked. Then, half running, half stumbling, she threw herself into him. He didn't see the blade she had hidden in her shorts. But he sure felt it as she sank it into his belly.

What a sight!

He stumbled backwards, gasping, looking at the wound, then up at her, as surprised as the rest of us. She was gasping hard, too. They stood a moment, bleeding, trying to clear their heads . . . as we kept shouting and cheering them on.

Then, with an energy from who knows where, the girl scooped up her broadsword from the sand and raced at him, shrieking like a crazed animal.

He tried to spin, to dodge, but she slammed it down into his left shoulder, so powerfully you could hear the joint crack and separate. And blood. So much we thought, we hoped, he'd lost the whole arm.

But it was still there. Barely. It didn't matter. He was exhausted, overcome, and fell to his knees.

That's when the lights in the arena went red. That's when we resumed chanting, "Kill! Kill! Kill!"

The girl staggered toward him, barely able to walk. He looked up. Too weak to move. To care.

"Kill! Kill! Kill!"

"Brenda . . ." It was Andi yelling at me.

I didn't look at her. I couldn't. Not now. The strobe lights began flashing. The girl screamed, fighting to raise her sword. She nearly fell from the pain and fatigue.

The arena shook with our voices. "Kill! Kill! Kill!"

She finally got it over her head.

"Kill! Kill! Ki—"

"NOOO!"

I turned to see Cowboy leap from his seat and race toward the arena.

"Cowboy!" I shouted.

He jumped over the wall and dropped into the pit. Security guards streamed down the aisles.

"Cowboy!"

"STOP IT!" He shouted. He ran straight for the girl. "WHAT ARE YOU DOING? STOP IT!"

The crowd began to boo. But he didn't hear. Or care. He grabbed the sword from her. She was too dazed and confused to put up a fight.

"WHAT ARE YOU DOING?"

A dozen security people were clambering over the wall and dropping into the pit. The booing got louder. Cowboy threw the girl's sword to the ground. The lights came up. He turned to the kid who'd passed out, fallen face-first into the sand. Bleeding out.

The announcer's voice boomed: "Remain in your

seats! Please, remain in your seats!"

By the time Cowboy kneeled to the kid, Security was all over him.

"Remain in your seats. The show will resume shortly. Please remain in your seats."

The booing continued. And for good reason. Cowboy had ruined everything. The show was heading for its big climax and he ruined it.

And that's what shocked me. Not his actions, but my thoughts. *Ruined?* Really? Cowboy was trying to save someone's life. And I resented him? What was I thinking? What was going on?

"Brenda . . . Brenda . . ."

I turned to Andi, confused and feeling more than a little guilty.

"Your earplugs," she shouted.

"What?"

She pointed to her ears. "Your earplugs!"

I looked down at my hand. I was still holding them.

"Put them in your ears! Put the earplugs in your ears!"

It made no sense. But she looked so serious. I turned to the professor. He was pointing to the ones in his own ears. I frowned, then nodded and put them in. The guilt and confusion grew even stronger. What had happened?

Suddenly, I heard the crowd gasp and I looked back to the arena. Cowboy was helping the kid to his feet. There was still plenty of blood, but no more was coming from his arm. His stomach was in bad shape. So were his toes. But the gash in his shoulder, the one that had nearly severed his arm and bled him out?

It was gone. There was no sign of the slightest

injury.

Chapter 6

Our hotel looked just like one of those Hollywood postcards. Everything pink, big pool, lots of palm trees. The rooms were huge—kitchen, bar, big screen TV, white carpet, tub with Jacuzzi.

And mirrors. Everywhere mirrors.

Course, none of us could sleep after the show. Most of all me. So we were meeting in Andi's room.

I sat there sketching—the same monster like on the plane, only now I was making its tentacles stretch around something that was supposed to be the world. Daniel was out on the balcony playing his apps. Cowboy was watching some football game. Andi had gutted one of those ear plug things and was studying it. And the professor had his face stuck in a newspaper.

"So it was all in my head?" I said. "All that stuff I was feeling?"

"Yes and no," Andi said. "The signal broadcast

throughout the auditorium lowered your inhibitions by restricting activity in a specific area of your frontal lobe."

The professor spoke without looking up. "Not entirely dissimilar to the fungus that attacked Andi and myself in Florida."

"But we killed all that," I said. "With that blue light."

"As far as we know," Andi said.

"Then how could—"

"Seriously?" The professor folded up his paper. "You don't think they could have found a different transporting mechanism by now? Something far more elegant?"

I added, "And more subtle. I didn't become some crazed zombie like you and Andi. I didn't think I was part of a universal mind."

"Nevertheless, your resistance toward violence was dramatically decreased."

"More than decreased. I really wanted to see that kid killed."

Andi nodded and quoted, "'The outlook on any morality can be changed through TV viewing.'"

"Another study?" I said.

"J.L. Singer. Yale University."

"And those ear plugs?"

She pushed them aside, taking a break. "They were designed to cancel out the signal. We all wore them . . . except you."

"So they plan on broadcasting that signal into every home in America?"

She shook her head. "The frequency is too high for the bandwidth assigned to television."

"Then, why—"

"Aw, shucks."

We turned to see Cowboy drop to his knees. He grabbed his Coke can which had fallen and was spilling all over the white carpet. "I didn't even touch the thing. It fell over all by itself."

Before we could respond, the big screen TV flickered and switched to that clip from *Superman* we'd seen before. It only lasted a second before going back to Cowboy's game.

"Oh brother," Cowboy sighed. "Again?"

Another flicker. This time to the *Rocky* movie. Then to the DiCaprio spinning top.

Cowboy pressed the remote again, then again, but nothing changed. "What's with the TV's in this city?" he complained.

Another flicker. Now we were watching that flying telephone booth show. Another flicker and it was *The Hunger Games*.

"It's identical to what we witnessed in the control room," the professor said. "And the limo ride."

Now we were watching that cartoon show with the talking ants. Then the newer, *Rocky* movie.

"Same order, too," Cowboy said.

"Are we certain of that?" I said.

"Here, let me check." Cowboy pulled out his smart phone as the TV repeated itself, starting with the *Superman* movie. "I was videoing them pillars, remember?" He brought up his recorded video and crossed over to us. "Hang on."

He fast forwarded through us sitting in the limo, then the pillars until he finally came to the first clip. It was the *Superman* movie. He pressed pause and waited for the same clip to reappear on the big screen TV. Once it did, he hit play and we watched his phone and the TV as the cycle began again. In perfect sync.

Andi picked up a pencil and paper and began writing.

"Do you believe there is some sort of pattern?" The professor asked.

She shrugged. "Only one way to find out."

Cowboy's phone stopped, but the TV repeated itself.

"Then please," the professor sighed, "do us a favor and at least put that on mute."

Cowboy obliged. But the images kept appearing and reappearing. I glanced over to Daniel on the balcony. He couldn't care less. Just kept on playing his game. Andi kept working, filling up one sheet, ripping it off, and starting another.

"Maybe they're like years or dates," Cowboy said. "Some secret code, like when you put all the numbers together they say something."

"To what purpose?" the professor said.

Cowboy shrugged.

"Or maybe it's not a pattern at all," I said.

Andi answered without looking up. "Everything's a pattern. Whether it's useful or not, there are always patterns."

Cowboy looked longingly at the screen, obviously not thrilled about missing his game. "Maybe I should call the front desk. See if they got another TV."

"Not yet," Andi said.

Cowboy slumped back into his seat. This was some kind of link. We all knew it. And the sooner Andi figured it out (and we all knew she would), the sooner we'd know what was going on.

I waited another cycle or two before I grabbed my pad and went back to sketching. The professor picked up his paper. And Cowboy eventually got up and joined Daniel on the balcony.

The TV never stopped repeating itself. It was back to the spinning top for the thousandth time when there was a knock on the door. We all looked up. Another knock. More impatient. I went over to answer, hesitated, then opened it to see Norman Anderson, the producer.

"What are you doing here?" I said.

He just stood there, staring down at his cell phone.

"What?" I repeated.

Without a word he turned the phone to face me. It was playing the same video Cowboy had shown us—starting off with brief shots of us in the limo, followed by the airport pillars, and finally the flickering clips on the limo's TV.

Cowboy stepped back into the room. "Hey, that's mine," he said. "I filmed that."

"You sent it to him?" I asked.

"Nobody sent me anything." Anderson did not sound happy. "It's playing all by itself. Has been the past ninety minutes." That's when he spotted our big screen TV playing the same images. Without an invitation, he stepped inside.

"Oh brother," Cowboy said. He'd pulled out his own phone and was staring at it. "This doesn't make sense."

"Now what?" the professor said.

"My video. I didn't touch nothing, but now it's gone. Erased. All of it. Now I just got this." He turned his phone around so we could see that the screen was filled with bright red letters—a single word that read: "SINCERELY." And below that a capital letter. "S."

Anderson looked down at his phone and swore. If he was unhappy before, he was downright livid now. He turned the screen back to us. It had the same word, "SINCERELY," in the same red letters. And, at the bottom, the same capital letter, "S."

I felt my own phone vibrate and frowned. Six people in the world have my cell number. (I like my privacy.) And half of them were in this room.

I pulled it out and, sure enough, there was the word "SINCERELY" followed by an "S."

"Who's S?" Cowboy asked.

Nobody had a clue.

"This is all a bit too melodramatic for my tastes," the professor said. "If the party wishes to leave us a message, they should at least have the courtesy to give us his or her name."

"Unless . . ." Andi stared at her latest sheet of paper.

"Unless what?" I said.

"Unless he didn't want his identity to be traced."

"Who?" Anderson said. "What are you talking about?"

Andi motioned to the big screen TV. She waited for the *Superman* scene to come around. When it did, she simply said, "*Superman.*"

"I was hoping for something less obvious," the professor said drolly.

Andi ignored him. "I don't know why I didn't see it earlier."

"A pattern?" I said.

She nodded. "And the professor is right, it is obvious." She turned to the TV screen and waited for the cycle to begin again. When it got there, she said, "*Superman* begins with the letter "S."

The screen flickered and switched to the *Rocky* movie.

"*Rocky* begins with the letter R."

The screen switched to the spinning top.

"T is for top," I said.

"Perhaps. But if we're naming movies . . ."

"*Inception*," Cowboy said. That's from *Inception*."

Andi nodded. "I is for *Inception*." The screen switched to the flying telephone booth. "And this is the British TV series, "*Dr. Who*."

"D," Cowboy said. "For *Doctor Who*."

The image switched again.

"*The Hunger Games*," I said. "T."

"Except most people drop the first word when it's as common as *the*," Andi said. "So let's consider this one an H."

Next, came the cartoon with the talking ants. No one had a clue except the professor. "That's *Antz*," he said. "My nephew loved that movie. Couldn't get enough of it. He's now an entomologist."

"A is for *Antz*, Andi said.

The *Rocky* scene came back on. "And we're back to R," I said.

Andi nodded. "But a different one."

"That's your pattern?" the professor groused. "Random letters?"

"Not so random." Andi looked back to the TV as the scenes cycled again, starting with the *Superman* clip. This time she called out each letter as the scene appeared: "S . . . R . . . I . . . D . . . H . . . A . . . R."

"That's no word," Anderson said.

"Sridhar!" I half spoke, half whispered. "The kid from our first mission. The one at the Institute who did the psychic dreaming."

"Lucid Dreaming," the professor corrected.

"He's doing this?" I turned back to Andi, waiting for her to answer. She didn't have to. Suddenly the TV fritzed out. Instead of movie clips we were back to watching Cowboy's football game. On the screen the crowd had leapt to their feet, cheering and clapping . . . as if someone had just scored an important goal.

Chapter 7

"So you've been fighting these supposed bad guys, this Gate, for how long?" Anderson asked.

"Long enough to know they don't play nice," I said.

"Such as?"

Cowboy answered, "Flying orbs, deadly molds—"

"And mind games." Andi sounded a little sheepish, no doubt thinking of her last encounter with them in Florida. "They're pretty good at those."

"No argument there," I said, thinking back to my own experience at the show.

We'd been sitting around Andi's hotel table for the last hour, explaining what we knew. Anderson listened carefully. He wasn't showing any of his cards, but you could tell he was interested. And concerned.

Finally he asked, "Why?"

"Why what?" I said

"What's their purpose?"

The professor answered. "That, my good man, is

the million dollar question. They appear to want some sort of control. World control. As in dominance."

"Like in the end times," Cowboy said.

We looked at him.

"You know, like it says in the Bible."

Anderson turned to the professor who said, "Not everybody is as gullible as our young friend here, but it does give one pause."

"And this Sridhar person?"

"A boy we tried to help. One who apparently feels compelled to reconnect."

"By jamming TVs, cell phones, and monitors?" Anderson asked.

"And maybe more," Andi said. "Do you remember what happened to your coffee in the control room?" She turned to me. "Or the water glass in the cafeteria?"

"Or my Coke can right here in this room," Cowboy added.

Andi nodded and pointed to the TV. "If he is indeed lucid dreaming, then maneuvering something with so little mass as electrons or as fluid as water would be the easiest way to impact our own world."

Anderson looked at her skeptically. "Lucid dreaming?"

"A technique first developed by the Department of Defense."

"*Supposedly* developed," the professor corrected.

Andi ignored him. "Select soldiers with psychic propensities were trained to send their souls out of their bodies while sleeping."

"To what purpose?"

"To spy on enemy facilities.

"You're not serious."

"It's documented."

"In part," the professor said.

"And it worked?" Anderson asked.

"According to the records. Though with some serious side effects."

"Like running into demons and stuff," Cowboy said.

Anderson threw him a glance and looked back to Andi. "And you think that's what this Sridhar fellow is doing, trying to get our attention?"

I spoke up. "The last time we saw him, Sridhar was being trained to work for the Gate."

Anderson quietly nodded. He looked out the sliding glass door to the balcony, thinking.

"So why did you come here?" Andi asked him.

I added, "Other than irritation over some cellphone malfunction?"

Cowboy interrupted. "If it's 'bout what I did at your show, I'm real sorry. But that boy, you could see he was hurt real bad. Like he was gettin' ready to check out."

"Which you may have noticed was the entire point of the show," the professor added drolly. "

Cowboy looked down and shrugged.

Anderson stared at the big guy a long moment. Finally he spoke, quietly. "What you did tonight, that was some trick."

"Not his first," Andi said.

Cowboy tried again. "Like I said, I'm real sorry, but—"

Anderson held up his hand. "No, no. What I saw you do, it was a lot more substantive than anything we were doing. Than anything I've ever done."

"So why are you here?" Andi repeated.

He took a breath, then answered. "Those pillars at the airport, the ones on our phones? I believe they're connected to your Gate . . . and my show."

"Leviathan."

I turned to see that Daniel had entered the room. He stood in front of the table holding up my sketch pad. The one with the monster and tentacles. He repeated the word: "Leviathan."

The professor turned back to Anderson. "Explain."

Anderson nodded to Daniel. "I'm not sure about that. But there are some things you should know." He hesitated a moment, then continued. "I think it's best I show you."

Chapter 8

Forty minutes later, courtesy of another limo ride, we were at St. Bartholomew's Medical Center. It was pretty close to the airport. I stayed outside a minute or two to catch a smoke. When I joined the others they were having coffee with some doctor kid, barely out of puberty, rich, and entitled. I was not a fan.

"Yeah, June thirtieth, hard to forget." The kid took a sip of vending machine coffee and made a face. Obviously not the gourmet roast he was used to. "Starting around one in the morning we had a huge rush. Stabbings, gang bangers, gun shots, rapes. You name it. And not just the usual minorities and lowlifes." He turned to me. "No offense."

I was liking him even less.

"And?" Anderson said. The kid looked at him and Anderson explained. "What you were telling me earlier. About the location."

"Oh, yeah. This was the crazy part. Every one of them had either been passing through LAX or lived near it."

We traded looks.

"These people," I said. "Any way we could talk to some of them?"

"That was nearly six weeks ago. Everyone's been released by now."

"What about addresses?" Andi asked.

"Doctor-patient confidentiality." He thought a moment. "But . . . we still have one with us. Least until we ship her off to happy acres."

"Pardon me?" the professor said.

"A nursing home. Soon as she gets out of here, her kids are sending her to a raisin farm."

My affection for him was not increasing.

"She'd been in an auto accident. Severe head trauma."

"Could we see her?" Anderson asked.

"This time of night? No way."

"Right." Anderson nodded. "Of course."

We sat in silence. I was still trying to piece it all together. What did the violence have to do with the Gate? The pillars? I glanced at Daniel. With Leviathan?

Anderson wasn't quite done. "Listen," he said to Doc Kid. "I got those new headshots of your niece."

"Yeah?"

"Getting prettier by the day. Fact there's a pilot

coming up that we just might be able to use her in."

"No kidding?"

"Of course there's a hundred other kids wanting the part, too."

"Right. Of course."

It seemed a strange topic to bring up now. But Anderson wasn't a top producer by accident. "About this older patient," he said. "You're sure there's no way we could wake her? Just talk with her for a couple minutes?"

The kid snorted. "They'd have my head."

Anderson nodded. "Right." He paused, then added, "Too bad."

Another pause. Longer. Cowboy, who hated any silence for over five seconds, was about to speak when I caught his eye and motioned for him to stay quiet. Something was up.

Finally Kid Doc cleared his throat. "When did you say those auditions were coming up?"

"Hm? Oh, next week."

He nodded.

Anderson took a sip of coffee, then added, "Sure is a cutie."

"Yeah," the kid said.

"Yeah," Anderson agreed.

Another pause.

"Listen." Kid Doc rose from his chair. "Why don't you hang here a minute. Let me see what I can do."

"About?"

"The raisin."

"But you just said—"

"I know, I know, but if there's some way to help you out . . ."

"That would be great," Anderson said. "I mean if

it doesn't jeopardize your position."

"This time of night? No one will know." He turned and started for the hallway. "Let me see what I can do."

He disappeared and I turned to Anderson. "You're good."

"Good?" he said. "I'm the best."

"But what's that got to do with them pillars?" Cowboy asked.

"Hang on," Anderson said. "We just might find out."

Twenty minutes later we were on the third floor talking to an elderly Mrs. Whitaker. Eighty, if she was a day.

"Lands sakes," she said. "It was the strangest thing. Sometimes when I can't sleep, which is a lot these days, I go driving. I was on Century Boulevard and this young fellow cut me off. Right in front of me. Didn't even look back. I think he was black." She turned to me. "No offense."

From her, I didn't mind.

"I didn't even honk at him. I just scowled. Real hard. Like this." She squinted, losing her eyes in folds of skin.

"And then?" the professor asked.

"And then he made one of those obscene hand gestures, like young folks do. And I got so mad. I can't explain it, but he really got my blood to boiling. Worse I can remember in a long time. So I gunned it. And at the next intersection, when he slowed to make a turn, I slammed into him. Hard. Bamb! And boy, oh boy, did it feel good. And I would have done it again, you know . . . if I'd still been conscious."

"You just sped up and hit him?" Andi asked.

"That's right."

"Couldn't help yourself?" the professor said.

"Oh, I'm sure I could. But I didn't want to. That's the strange part. I wanted to knock the stuffings out of him. So I did."

I couldn't help but nod. After what I went through during last night's show, I knew exactly what she was feeling. Only with me it hadn't been anger. It was the thrill of violence. I knew it was wrong. And I could have looked away and calmed down if I really wanted. But the thing is, I didn't want.

When we were done we thanked her and started for the hallway.

"Young man?"

Cowboy, Anderson, even the professor turned around. But she was talking to Anderson. "The doctor tells me you're a TV producer."

"Yes, ma'am."

"Well, I did a little acting. In community theater, I mean. So if you ever need a feisty, go-get 'em gal that's middle-aged, look me up, okay?"

He smiled. "Middle-aged?"

"Or older. There's lots of things you can do with makeup to make me look older."

"Yes, ma'am. I'll keep that in mind."

We did our best not to smile as we turned and exited into the hallway. As we approached the elevators, Anderson looked to me. "So what she was feeling . . . sound familiar?"

I nodded. "Sure did."

"But what's that got to do with those pillars at LAX?" Cowboy asked.

We arrived at the elevators and Anderson hit the button. "It's about time you see."

Chapter 9

We were back in the limo heading for LAX. Anderson still wasn't playing all his cards. Not that I blamed him. Truth is, if he'd told us what he knew, we wouldn't have believed him anyway.

But we'd find out soon enough.

Meanwhile, Andi had found something on her tablet. "Hey guys, check this out. In the early morning hours of June 30, Precinct 14 reported an unusual number of arrests—everything from DUI's to convenience store robberies, to date rapes, you name it."

"Precinct 14?" I said.

She nodded. "LAX is in that jurisdiction."

"It's just what the kid doctor said."

"And more." We turned to the professor. "If Andrea's information is correct, then crimes of rage weren't the only offenses being perpetrated."

Anderson agreed. "They were crimes of impulse, lack of self-control."

I nodded. "I could have turned from last night's fight any time I wanted."

"But you chose not to."

"I knew it was wrong. I knew I shouldn't. But I didn't care."

"Because we were able to reduce the inhibition impulses of your brain." He took a breath. "At least that's what the tests showed."

"You've run tests on it?" the professor asked.

"Not us. An independent firm. One hired by an organization that likes to keep a low profile. Someone we've already discussed beforehand. Your friend and mine . . ." He let the phrase hang until Andi finished it.

"The Gate," she said.

He nodded. We all sat in silence absorbing the information. A moment later he spotted something outside. "Here." He rapped on the glass separating us from the driver. "Stop here." The driver lowered the window and Anderson repeated, "Stop here."

"But sir, there is no parking—"

"*Stop here!*"

"Yes, sir."

The driver slowed and pulled to the side. Before the limo even stopped, Anderson was out the door. He crossed the four-lane road and headed toward one of the pillars. It rose from the grassy medium, about twenty feet tall and glowed purple.

We got out of the car and followed. Even at three in the morning there was traffic—complete with honking horns and irate drivers motioning us to get out of their way. By the time we arrived, the pillar was turning a pale blue. I tapped its side. It was made of thick, milky plastic. The color came from lights glowing inside.

Anderson knelt down at its base and pushed away some of the landscaped bushes. At the very bottom a metal box was attached. Rectangular, two by three feet. Camouflage green. A small amber light glowed on the top. Beside the light was a digital screen.

"And what precisely are we looking upon?" the professor asked.

Andi knelt to join Anderson as the man explained. "These are the same emotional generators we have stationed around the arena back at the studio."

"Emotional generators?" I said.

"Yes."

"That's what got Miss Brenda all worked up?" Cowboy asked.

Anderson nodded. "They are designed to create and amplify the signal that reduces our inhibitions."

"The signal that those ear devices blocked," Andi said.

"Correct. They generate the signal, then cycle it from generator to generator, amplifying it until it is strong enough to direct at the audience."

Like the old crystal lasers," the professor said. "Aligning and reflecting light frequencies back and forth until they're powerful enough to be released."

"If you say so. The point is, once they'd been thoroughly tested, my production company ordered six of the units."

"And?" I asked.

"We were charged for twenty-one."

"That's a big difference," Cowboy said.

"I put our production accountant on it and she said the other fifteen were donated to the Light and Luminescence Corporation."

"The who?" I said.

"The company in charge of maintaining these columns.

"Why would they need fifteen generators?" Cowboy said.

"How many columns do they have here?" Andi asked.

Anderson looked at her. "Fifteen."

The professor spoke up. "So your theory is that these generators are what effected the people in this area on June thirtieth."

Anderson nodded. "Lowering their inhibition and self-control."

"And this amber light?" Andi pointed to the little light on the box.

"It's in standby mode."

With effort, the professor stooped for a closer look. "Meaning what, exactly?"

"It's ready to transmit any time."

"Now?" I asked.

"Or tomorrow, or the next day, or—"

Pointing to a toggle switch on the side, the professor interrupted. "Then I suggest we simply turn off the contraption and—"

"Professor, I wouldn't—"

Too late. He flipped the switch to the *off* position. Well, you'd think it should have been *off*, but the light turned from amber to bright green. At the same time the little digital screen beside it lit up with the numbers:

15.00.00

which immediately started counting down:

14:59:59
14:59:58
14:59:57

The professor swore, flipping the switch up, then down, then up again. Nothing.

14:59:52
14:59:51
14:59:50

I heard a quiet hum and looked up. Something like a miniature satellite dish, no bigger than a cereal bowl, was rising out of the top of the pillar.

"That can't be good," I said.

"Or that." Andi pointed across the way to the next column. A similar dish was also rising, pointing the same direction. And beyond that, another column with a rising dish.

"What is it?" Cowboy asked.

"Microwave," Andi answered.

"What are they pointing at?" I said. "They're all pointing the same direction."

Andi pulled out her cell phone.

The professor was still on his knees, fighting the switch. "Andrea!"

She pointed her phone up at the dish.

"Triangulating now."

"What's going on?" Cowboy repeated.

No one answered.

"I'm too low," Andi said. "I've got to get a better angle. I've got to—"

Suddenly our cell phones rang. All of them. I reached into my pocket and pulled mine out. On the screen was an old, stone church.

Cowboy's must have showed the same. "A church?" he said.

I nodded and looked to the professor who was also fumbling with his phone "Professor?"

"Yes," he answered. "Mine is a church as well."

"St. Johns," Anderson said. He was staring at his own phone. "The abandoned church on West Manchester."

"You recognize it?" Andi asked.

Without a word, he turned and started back across the street.

"You know this place?" the professor called.

Anderson shouted back. "It's six blocks from here."

I glanced at the digital clock.

14:57:18
14:57:17
14:57:16

We traded looks. Then started back through the traffic to join him.

Chapter 10

"And of all the churches in Los Angeles, how did you recognize this particular one?" the professor asked.

"The news," Anderson said. "It's been deserted a couple years now. Developers want to tear it down but the city keeps blocking them. Very strange."

"What's strange about that?" Cowboy asked.

"The city of Los Angeles fighting to keep a church? You really aren't from around here, are you?"

We'd parked the limo a block away. Anderson's suggestion to draw less attention. The closer we got to the place, the creepier it looked. Weeds, ivy overgrowing old stone walls. The steeple seemed a bit taller than normal. Other than that, nothing was unusual.

"So how we getting in?" I asked.

Anderson motioned to Cowboy. "With his size and the condition of those doors, it shouldn't be a problem."

But it was a problem. From the sidewalk the doors looked like old, rotting wood. But when we got closer and checked them out, we saw they were actually metal. Steel painted to look like old wood.

"Weird," Cowboy said.

I motioned to the small electronic box beside the doors. "Is that going to be a problem?"

Andi was already opening some program in her cell phone. "Shouldn't be." She grinned as she held the phone against the lock and it began beeping real fast. "One of my favorite apps."

We waited a half minute until the lock clicked and the beeping stopped. She pocketed the phone and pushed open the door. Immediately an alarm sounded, complete with flashing lights.

"Tank!" Andi called over it. "Will you take care of that?"

"Me?"

She motioned to the control panel on the wall not far from the door. He stepped up to it, gave it a good, hard look, then whacked it off the wall with his fist.

Everything stopped.

He grinned back at Andi. "One of *my* favorite apps."

The inside of the church was anything but a church. It had more monitors and walls of electronic junk than three or four of Anderson's TV control rooms put together. Geek heaven for Andi. She left us and begin checking it out.

There was one thing we all recognized. On the bottom of each monitor was the same type of digital read out we'd seen at the airport:

00:09:01

"What does it mean?" Cowboy asked.

"I don't know," I said. "But I'm not liking it."

Oh, and there was one other thing we recognized .

. .

"Greetings."

We spun around to see a way too familiar guy in a three piece suit. He'd just strolled out from behind one of the walls of computers.

"Dr. Trenton?" Cowboy gasped.

"Who?" Anderson said.

Trenton continued like he hadn't heard. "No doubt you've noticed you are on private property."

"Dr. Trenton," Cowboy repeated. "Remember us?"

"He can't hear you," the professor said. "I suspect he is a holographic image. As before."

And he was right. Trenton just kept on talking like he never heard a word. The guy pulled a pocket watch from his vest. "You have exactly fifteen seconds to remove yourself from the premises."

I turned to Anderson and explained. "He's from the Psychic Research Institute. A training ground for the Gate."

"Was," the professor said.

"'Til we kinda destroyed it," Cowboy said.

"Ten seconds."

Anderson took a step toward the hologram. "Fascinating." And then another step.

"Five seconds."

Anderson nodded. "He's simply a pre-recorded

display."

"Well, all right." Trenton closed his watch. "But please remember, you have been warned."

Suddenly, one of those floating orbs we'd seen in Florida appeared from behind Trenton. It was blue and the size of a softball.

Anderson took a step back. "What the—"

"Relax," I said, "it can't hurt you." More softly I added, "I hope."

Because I was the first to speak, it flew right at me and stopped three or so feet away. It hovered at eye level. I steeled myself, refusing to flinch. Hoping I sounded tough, I said, "And what do you want?"

A pencil-thin beam of light shot out and scanned my face.

"Andi?" I said. But she was out of sight, examining equipment. "Professor?"

A second later the beam stopped and Trenton turned toward me. "Well, Brenda Barnick, so good to see you again."

I glanced to the professor for help.

"Facial recognition," he said.

As soon as the professor spoke, the orb darted to his face and began scanning him. When it had finished, Trenton turned to him. "And Dr. McKinney. What a treat to see you as well."

"I'm sure you're thrilled."

Anderson turned to me. "What's going on?"

The orb flew to his face and began scanning. You could see the muscles in Anderson's jaw tighten, but taking his cue from me and the professor, he refused to back down.

Cowboy started to speak but I motioned for him to keep quiet. Daniel, too. I figured the fewer of us they knew were here, the better.

When the scan finished, Trenton stood a moment like he was thinking. Then his face lit up. "Well, hello there—Mr. Norman Anderson, the famous TV producer. Good to see you, sir. You've been so helpful to us these many years. However, and I don't mean to be rude, these grounds are private property and I am afraid you must leave. At once."

One thing I'd learned about Anderson, like me he wasn't great at taking orders. "And if I don't?"

Trenton gave no answer.

Anderson looked around the room. "What's all this about? And those extra generators at the pillars. The ones you've charged to my show's account. What exactly are you doing here?"

Trenton ignored him. "I believe there's somebody here who'd like to see you."

"Who? What are you talking about?"

Trenton just smiled. The floating orb shot back to him. He turned and disappeared behind the wall of computers with it following him.

Andi called from another bank of computers. "The generators are fully charged."

"They're what?" I said.

"The pillars have been building a charge. They've begun transmitting it to these storage units."

"That doesn't sound good," Cowboy said.

"It gets worse. The steeple on top of this roof? It appears to be some sort of an antenna."

"To receive the charge?" the professor said.

"And to transmit it. From what I can tell, when the signal is strong enough—when the countdown reaches zero—it's going to beam the signal to a satellite in geosynchronous orbit overhead which, in turn, will broadcast the signal over a specific area of the nation. I believe it to be the central states of the Midwest."

Before any of us could answer, two eight-year-old girls suddenly appeared from behind Trenton's wall of computers. Hair tangled, faces dirty, shirts ripped and torn, they ran toward us. They were chained together, foot to foot. One was blonde, the other was—

"Helsa!" Cowboy cried. And he was right. The girl was our friend from the parallel universe.

"Daddy!" the blonde shouted to Anderson. "Daddy!"

"Sophia!" Anderson cried. "Sweetheart!"

"Daddy!" The girl stumbled and fell to the floor, dragging Helsa down with her. "Daddy, help me!"

Anderson started toward her, but the professor grabbed his arm. "She's not here," he said. "It's a holographic image."

Anderson hesitated, then slowed to a stop.

"Daddy, you have to go!" the girl shouted. "You have to go *now* or they'll hurt us more."

"Hurt you? What have they done to you? Where are you?"

The girl didn't answer, only began to cry.

"Helsa!" Cowboy repeated.

But Helsa didn't answer, either.

"It's me, Tank," Cowboy said.

"She doesn't know you're here," the professor said. "The orb never saw you." To prove his point, he called out, "Helsa?"

Helsa turned to him.

The professor motioned to me and I did the same. "Helsa?"

She turned to me.

"Daddy, please!" the daughter cried again. "You've got to go!"

I frowned, trying to piece it together. No way did they know Anderson would break in. No way would they kidnap his daughter unless they knew in advance. But they couldn't know.

Daniel tugged on my arm. I looked down. He was pointing at the girls. "Shadows," he said.

"What?"

He kept pointing. "The shadows, they're different."

I turned back to the girls.

He repeated, "They're different."

Then I saw it. The light hitting Helsa was coming from the right. The light hitting Sophia was from the front.

"Sweetheart," Anderson shouted. "Where are you? What have they done to you?"

"Daddy, please, you've got to go."

I called over to Anderson. "She's not there."

He answered, "Yeah, I get it, holographic image. But they've got her somewhere."

"That's impossible," the professor said. "The odds of them knowing you would be with us are—"

I interrupted. "Photoshop." They turned to me and I explained. "They grabbed a video of your daughter, probably off the internet. They computer generated her to talk and look at us, but they don't have her. She's not there."

"Daddy, please go."

The professor nodded. "Your daughter is safe and sound in Maui."

"And Helsa?" Cowboy asked.

"The same," I said, hoping I was right.

"Daddy! Daddy, you've got to go!"

Anderson looked from me to the professor, then back to the girls. He was a media guy. It should have made perfect sense. Then again, he was also a dad. He reached for his cell phone. "Well, there's one way to find out. I'll give them a call and see—"

Suddenly every monitor in the room lit up. Just one word. Two letters. Different fonts, different sizes, but the same two letter word over and over again, filling the screens:

NO! no! NO! no! No! nO! NO! no! NO! no!
No! nO! NO! no! NO! no! No! nO! NO! NO!
no! NO! no! No! nO! no! NO! no! No! nO!
NO! no! NO! no! No! nO! NO! no! NO! no!

"What?" Anderson said. "What's going on?"

The words disappeared. They were immediately replaced by the same clips we'd seen so many times before:

Superman, Rocky, Inception, Doctor Who, The Hunger Games, Antz, Rocky. Superman, Rocky, Inception, Doctor Who, Hunger Games, Antz, Rocky . . .

"Stop dialing!" I shouted to Anderson. "It's—" I started to say Sridhar's name, but caught myself. "Our friend! He's telling you to stop!"

But the girl continued pleading. "Daddy, please. You've got to go!"

Anderson ignored me and went back to dialing.

The screens returned to:

NO! no! NO! no! No! nO! NO! no! NO! no!
No! nO! NO! no! NO! no! No! nO! NO! NO!
no! NO! no! No! nO! no! NO! no! No! nO!
NO! no! NO! no! No! nO! NO! no! NO! no!

Anderson entered the last number.

"What did you do?" Andi shouted from her computers. She sounded panicky. "What did you just do!"

I shouted back, "He's calling his daughter. Why?"

"His signal, it's overriding the satellite's signature."

"Meaning?"

"It intercepted the microwave. It's shifted it to his phone, to all our phones."

Anderson looked at me, then slowly disconnected.

"He's hung up," I called.

"It doesn't matter, it's still receiving!"

"His?"

"Ours. They're all hot spots. Receiving and transmitting."

I threw a look over to the monitors.

00:04:27

"The clock says we've still got four and a half minutes."

"That's for the satellite uplink. But our own phones . . . every phone in this proximity is receiving the signal now. And transmitting it! It's happening now!"

Chapter 11

The professor smashed his cell phone onto the floor. It shattered into a half dozen pieces.

"What are you doing?" I shouted.

"If Andi is correct, I am destroying the transmitter device. Each of you must do the same. You must destroy your phones."

He reached for mine and I pushed him away. "You can't be sure. These things are expensive."

"If you had a modicum of intelligence you would understand."

"I understand just fine."

He reached for it again and I shoved him away harder. "You're not always right. What makes you so right?"

"Having more than a tenth grade education

increases my odds."

I shot him a glare.

"Or is it ninth grade, I forget."

He reached for my phone again and I punched him in the gut. It surprised me as much as it did him. But it felt pretty good. So I hit him again. That's when Cowboy grabbed my arm and spun me around.

"Stop it!" the big lug shouted. "Stop it right now!" I tried to twist free, but he was twice my size. "I'm so sick of you two fightin' all the time! You need to grow up!"

The professor righted himself, testing his stomach. "Maybe if our resident bag lady could resort to a more civilized way of expressing her—"

"Shut up! Both of you. Just shut up!"

I stared at Cowboy. I'd never heard a mean thing come from his mouth. And the professor. Yeah, we had some mutual disrespect goin', but he'd never resorted to name calling. And I'd never dreamed of hitting him.

"It's the generators," Andi shouted. "They're effecting us."

"Well, fix it!" Anderson yelled. "You're supposed to be the electronic genius."

Cowboy let go of my arm and turned on him. "You don't talk that way to Andi. She's good, and smart, and sweet and—"

She cut him off. "And not the slightest bit interested in you."

He turned to her, obviously hurt.

She continued. "Seriously, what do I have to do to get through that thick skull of yours?" She turned to Anderson. "But you . . ." She smiled coyly. "You have the brains *and* the bod." Her voice softened. "Not to mention power. I like powerful men. If you ever feel you want a little companionship, intellectual or otherwise, just let me know and I'll—"

"Please," Anderson scorned, "I'm not interested in children." His gaze shifted to me. "But real women—street smart with experience—now that's something I could get into. Really get into."

"Dream on," I said.

"I'm serious." He stepped closer. "With all the bimbos around, it's been a long time since I've had myself a real woman. And I'm betting, since you've had a real man." He took my arm.

I looked down at his grip then glared back up at him. He didn't get the message. I tried to break free, but he grabbed my other arm and pulled me toward him. I head-butted him. That message he did get. He staggered backwards. But only for a second.

"Yeah," he sneered, "a scrapper. I like that."

He came at me again. I threw a punch, but he grabbed my arm and pulled me into him, tight. I tried getting away, using my elbows and knees, but he had me in too close. I shouted. Swore. Turned to the others for help.

But the professor just stood there, arms crossed, smirking away. Cowboy was no better. Fact is, as he watched Anderson grab and grope, he got ideas of his own. Inspired, he turned and headed for Andi.

For the briefest second Anderson left himself open. I made my move. I jerked my knee into his groin. He groaned and stumbled away. He wanted a scrapper, he got a scrapper.

I threw a look to Daniel. He just sat on the floor, lost in the screams and explosions of his game app.

"Daniel!"

He ignored me.

"Daniel!"

He scooted around 'til his back was to me. He couldn't be bothered.

I spun back to the monitors.

00:02:28

"I told you," Andi said, "I'm not interested!"

I turned to see Cowboy had backed her against one of the terminals. He leaned over her awkwardly. "One little kiss, it ain't gonna hurt nothin'."

The professor laughed and I shot him a look.

He shrugged. "Quite a show."

I might of hit him again, just for spite, if Anderson wasn't coming at me. He arrived just in time for me to land a good fist to his jaw. Probably broke my hand, but it sure felt good. Too good. Like hitting every man who'd ever hurt and abused me. Anderson swore up a storm. I answered by punching him again. This time his nose. It began bleeding. A real gusher. He backed up. Too bad, 'cause I really wanted to keep going.

And I wasn't the only one.

"C'mon," Cowboy hovered over Andi, practically drooling.

But she wasn't backing down. "What about *no* doesn't that hick brain of yours get?"

"Lots a girls want me," he said.

She laughed.

"I'm serious. But I ain't ever given in."

"Trust me, your record's safe with me."

Another alarm went off. A piercing buzz. I looked back to the monitors. The numbers at the bottom had turned red:

00:02:00

The buzzer stopped just in time for me to hear Daniel shouting, "Yes! Yes!" I turned to see him hunched over his game, totally lost in it.

Off in the distance there was a police siren. More than one.

The professor chuckled. "Should be another busy night." I turned to him and he continued. "I believe Andrea said *all* phones within the proximity."

"Professor McKinney! Brenda!"

I spun back to the monitors. The digital readout continued at the bottom of the screen, but above it was a face I'd not seen in months.

"Sridhar!"

"Yes, it is I." He glanced over his shoulder, then back to the camera. "Please, you must put an end to this behavior at once."

"Where are you?"

"I have but only a moment. You must overcome your impulses and shut down the equipment in the room and you must do so immediately."

"Actually," the professor said, "it's proving to be quite the entertainment."

"In just over a minute, the entire central portion of your country will be exposed."

"To what?" I said.

"To what you are now experiencing. The loss of inhibition. People will become subject to their desires with little regard of the outcome."

"That's their worry," Andi said.

"Please," Sridhar said, "you must find the strength

to restrain your desires. You must overcome your impulses and shut down the equipment."

The professor snickered. I grinned. We both knew the chances were next to none.

But the kid continued. "Andi, inside the panel to your left are several cables. If you would disconnect them—"

Andi cut him off. "Do you have any idea how sick I am of people always telling me what to do? Just because I'm brilliant I'm expected to fix everything at their command."

The professor countered. "Maybe if you had some backbone, people wouldn't feel compelled to take advantage of—"

"Shut up!" she snapped. "For once in your life just shut up!"

"Ooo." It was my turn to chuckle. "Look who's growing up."

"And you." She turned on me. "You think all that sarcasm makes you cool? Well, here's a little wake up call for—"

The alarm went off again. Only this time it didn't stop. The numbers below Sridhar read:

00:01:00

"One minute," Anderson shouted over the alarm. "This should get interesting."

As he spoke two other men showed up on Sridhar's monitor. They grabbed the boy and he shouted, "No! Let me go! This is not right! You must—"

"Sridhar!" I yelled.

"Let me go!" For a little guy, he put up quite the

73

fight. "Let me go! You must not—" until one of the goons slammed his head down onto the console. Hard.

"Sridhar!"

But it would take more than that to stop the kid. He was back up, blood streaming down his forehead, and shouting, "You must destroy that equipment. You must—"

The men yanked him out of his chair. He cried out until they hit him again. This time he went limp. Goon One dragged him off as Goon Two stuck his face into the camera. He fiddled with a switch and the screen went blank. Except for the readout below:

00:00:47

"This ain't good!" Cowboy yelled." I turned to him in surprise. His face was twisted, like he was fighting something. "Sridhar's right," he said, "we gotta do something."

"Actually, it's really quite amusing," the professor said.

"No. It's gonna get real bad. Out there, everywhere. It's going to get real bad for everybody."

Anderson smirked. "And that concerns you because?"

"Because? Because it ain't right. Because they're people. Kids, moms, dads. Every day people, just like you and me."

The sirens continued to approach.

Cowboy's face had grown shiny with sweat. Whatever was goin' on inside him was a lot. A real war. He looked to each one of us like we could help. Like we should want to.

"Are you telling me you don't want to see a little violence?" Anderson asked. "A little action?"

Cowboy closed his eyes, clenching his jaw, trying to drown out Anderson's words.

Anderson motioned to Andi. "You were pretty interested in a little action a second ago. I bet you still are."

The big guy looked to Andi. You could see the battle raging inside him.

Anderson continued. "I'm sure your God wouldn't mind. Just this once."

And that did it. Something inside Cowboy snapped. Switched on. The fight was still there, there was no missing it, but now there was something else. A tiny spark. A light that quickly grew. A strength. Brighter by the second.

Finally, he turned to Andi. "Those cables, where did he say they were?"

"You're not serious," she said.

Anderson agreed. "For the first time in your life you're free. Free to do anything you want. And you're trying to hold back, trying to hold us all back with some lame, religious—"

"No, sir." Cowboy continued growing stronger. "I know what freedom is, and this ain't it."

I glanced to the professor. He was looking down, scowling. Whatever Cowboy was saying, whatever he was doing, was obviously having an effect on the old man.

But not Andi. She stepped closer to Cowboy. "Maybe you just haven't experienced enough freedom." It was laughable, hearing her pretend to come on to him.

But it worked.

Cowboy swallowed. He shifted his weight.

She continued. "Isn't that what you want, Tank?" She stepped closer. "Isn't real freedom what we all want?"

He swallowed again. It looked like he was about to cave when, at the very last second, from who knows where, he found the strength to look away.

"Hey." She took his arm.

He ignored her and looked to the computers. "It's this panel here, right?"

I glanced to the monitors.

00:00:20

"Maybe." Andi stepped back in his way.

Cowboy took another breath. Then he reached out to her. As carefully as holding an armed bomb, he took her shoulders and gently moved her to the side.

It was touching. And somehow, in a way I can't explain . . . inspiring. Enough for me to feel a little of my own resolve starting to return.

He stooped down and looked into the back of the computer.

00:00:14

"There's so many cables," his voice echoed from inside. "Won't you help me?"

Andi must have felt something, too. Like the professor. Like me. Somehow his strength was feeding ours. She looked over to us. I didn't know what to say. And for once, neither did the professor. She frowned. She looked down at Cowboy. Then she knelt to join him.

00:00:09

"Could be those wires there," she said.
"These?" he asked.
"Yes."

00:00:05

"No! I'm wrong!" she said. "Try those. Those right there!"
He gave her a look.
She nodded.
He reached further inside—

00:00:01

—and gave a yank.
Nothing.
He yanked harder. Suddenly the console exploded with more sparks than the fourth of July.
Everything went dark.
And there in the darkness, as embarrassment over our words and our actions washed through us, we started coming back to our senses.
Police lights flooded through the windows. A moment later they were busting into the room. But it didn't matter. It was over.
It was over and, somehow, some way, we had won.

The next day gave a new meaning to the word *awkward*. Yeah, the police showed up that night with lots of arrests around the area, including busting us for breaking and entering. And, yeah, Anderson had to pull some strings and do some fast talkin' to get us free. (Like he said, he's good at what he does).

But the real truth is, it's like we all caught each other naked, with no clothes. Like we saw what we could really be like if you stripped away all our niceties. Course, we all apologized to each other, sayin' it really wasn't us. And, of course, we all knew we were lying. Because some where inside, some part of us really was feeling all that junk.

Anyways . . .

By late the next day, we were all loaded in the limo and headin' back to the airport, pretending everything was normal. Daniel was back to playing his apps, despite (or because of) the professor's criticism of my parenting skills. Andi was on the phone. I'd busied myself finishing up the sketch of that octopus monster thing. And the professor, as usual, was hiding behind his puffed-up intellect.

"A remarkable experience when you stop to think of it objectively," he said. "The possibilities when one's inhibitions are completely removed, when one is unfettered by moral restraint."

"Whatever it was," Cowboy said, "I didn't like it."

"You seemed fine with it for a time."

The big guy threw a nervous look to Andi who was still on the phone. "God didn't make morals for us to go around breakin' 'em," he said.

"Yes, well I'm afraid *God* had little to do with creating morality," the professor said. "Morals are merely the logical extension of man's attempt to keep our race from destroying itself—seeking what's best for the community rather than our own self-centered desires."

"I don't know about none of that," Cowboy said. "But I do know if it weren't for God, I'd never have had the strength to do what was right."

"Maybe," I said. "But seein' what you did, sure helped the rest of us."

The professor agreed. "Witnessing proper behavior can, indeed, instill and promote proper behavior. While witnessing improper behavior can often—"

"Make folks do bad," Cowboy said.

The professor nodded. "Which is precisely why the Gate wishes to control the media."

"They want to show folks doin' bad so others start doin' it."

I pointed at Andi. "What was it she quoted? Any moral can be changed through the media?"

"Leviathan," Daniel said.

I turned to him. "What's that?"

He didn't bother to look up from his game.

"Leviathan," Cowboy repeated. "It's in the Bible. Some sort of sea monster."

"With tentacles?" I asked.

Cowboy shrugged.

"With arms that can slither undetected into every mind and household in America," the professor added.

Daniel's game blasted with another burst of gun fire followed by the usual screams and explosions.

I glanced to the professor. He gave the usual disapproving arch of his eyebrow.

"Daniel?" I said.

He didn't hear.

"Daniel?"

Still nothing.

I sighed. The professor had been right way too many times on this trip. But I had to give him another one.

I reached over and took the game out of Daniel's hands."

"Hey!"

"Leviathan," I said.

He reached for it. "That's mine."

"You've played enough for now," I said.

"That's not fair."

"Welcome to life."

He folded his arms and slumped into a sulk. I did my best to avoid the professor's eyes.

A moment later Andi disconnected from her call. "Well," she said, "that's encouraging."

"What?" Cowboy asked.

"Anderson has shut down the show."

"That's fantastic," Cowboy said.

"Good news," I agreed.

"And the LAPD is investigating the placement of all the equipment inside the church and the generators around those pillars."

"Will it do any good?" I asked.

She shrugged. "Norman says the news channels have already gotten wind of it and—"

The professor chuckled. "Oh, Norman, is it now?"

I glanced to Cowboy, who pretended not to hear.

Andi continued. "Mr. Anderson casts a pretty big shadow in the town. More importantly, he has offered his services to us. He understands the Gate's influence, especially in its use of the media, and he's promised to do all he can to help stop them."

"That's great," Cowboy said, overdoing the enthusiasm a bit. "That probably means we'll see him again."

Andi nodded. "I hope so."

Cowboy said nothing and just looked out the window.

The professor took a deep breath. "And so, another battle has been won." Musing, he added, "Almost in spite of ourselves."

"But we still got the war," I said. "A big one. Seems there's nothing the Gate isn't messin' with."

Cowboy turned from the window. "But it ain't our job to worry about it, Miss Brenda." I looked over to him and he nodded at my sketch pad. "We just keep cuttin' off the tentacles that get shown to us. That's all we can do."

"What's the old child's riddle?" the professor asked. "'How do you eat an elephant?'"

We turned to him and he answered, "'One bite at a time.'" He looked back out the window as our limo pulled up to the curb. "That's how we shall destroy them." He repeated, as much for himself as for us . . . "One bite at a time."

We sat there in silence. Despite all we'd said and done to each other the night before, we'd never felt closer. Could be all the battles we'd been fighting together, the impossible enemy we were up against, or who knows what. Whatever it was, for that one brief moment, like it or not, we were family.

Finally, the professor opened his door and stepped out. The others followed. I lagged behind to get Daniel and all our stuff.

"Let's go, Barnick," the professor barked.

"Hang on." I turned to Daniel. "You got your hoodie? Those planes get cold."

He nodded and pulled out his sweatshirt. I checked the seats and floor for anything we might have left behind.

"Barnick."

"Hang on."

A moment later we crawled out. But the professor didn't let up. "Have you ever, for once in your entire life, been punctual?"

"You try lugging a kid all around," I snapped.

"A kid?" He motioned to the nearby porter to

handle his suitcases. "Don't tell me about children. I have four of them to look after. And there isn't a one of you who isn't more trouble than you are worth." He turned and started for the terminal "Let's go, people. The plane's waiting."

I slung my backpack over my shoulder and turned to Andi. "And . . . we're back."

She grinned and took Daniel's hand. "It sure looks that way."

"Yes it does," I muttered. "Yes, it does."

Soli Deo gloria.

OTHER BOOKS BY BILL MYERS

NOVELS
Child's Play
The Judas Gospel
The God Hater
The Voice
Angel of Wrath
The Wager
Soul Tracker
The Presence
The Seeing
The Face of God
When the Last Leaf Falls
Eli
Blood of Heaven
Threshold
Fire of Heaven

NON-FICTION
The Jesus Experience—Journey Deeper into the Heart of God
Supernatural Love
Supernatural War

CHILDREN BOOKS
Baseball for Breakfast (picture book)
The Bug Parables (picture book series)
Imager Chronicles (fantasy series)
McGee and Me (book/video series)
The Incredible Worlds of Wally McDoogle (comedy series)
Bloodhounds, Inc. (mystery series)

The Elijah Project (supernatural suspense series)
Secret Agent Dingledorf and His Trusty Dog Splat
  (comedy series)
TJ and the Time Stumblers (comedy series)
Truth Seekers (action adventure series)

TEEN BOOKS
Forbidden Doors (supernatural suspense)
  Dark Power Collection
  Invisible Terror Collection
  Deadly Loyalty Collection
  Ancient Forces Collection

For a complete list of Bill's books, sample chapters, and newsletter signup go to www.Billmyers.com Or check out his Facebook page: www.facebook.com/billmyersauthor.

Don't miss the other books in the Harbingers series wich can be purchased separately or in collections:

CYCLE ONE: INVITATION
The Call,
The House,
The Sentinels,
The Girl.

CYCLE TWO: MOSAIC
The Revealing
Infestation
Infiltration
The Fog

CPSIA information can be obtained at www.ICGtesting.com
Printed in the USA
LVOW10s2159240816

501735LV00014B/292/P